MW01448823

TO MY HUSBAND, BRANDON, WHO INSPIRED THIS BOOK... I AM SO EXCITED FOR YOU TO MAKE FISHING MEMORIES WITH OUR CHILDREN ONE DAY. THANK YOU FOR KEEPING MY CREATIVITY AND INNER CHILD ALIVE.

TO MY DAD, CARLOS, THANK YOU FOR ALL OF THE FISHING MEMORIES. FOR THE LESSONS, LAUGHS, AND FOR STEALING MY BASS. I LOVE YOU.

TO THE FAMILIES WHO WILL READ THIS WITH THEIR LITTLE ONES...

I HOPE THIS ENCOURAGES YOU TO KEEP FISHING.

THANK YOU FOR KEEPING THE MAGIC AND LOVE ALIVE WITH ME. I APPRECIATE YOU ALL MORE THAN YOU WILL EVER KNOW.
-CHALISE

ABCDEF
GHIJKL
MNOPQ
RSTUV
WXYZ

A

A IS FOR ANGLER,
A PERSON WHO
LOVES TO FISH!

B

B IS FOR BASS, OR THE BOAT I WANT TO RIDE IN!

C

C is for Croaker, Catfish, and Carp.

D

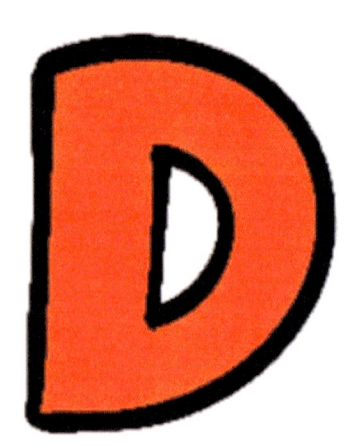

D IS FOR DRUM,
THEY MAKE NOISE
AND HAVE DISTINCT
MARKS.

E

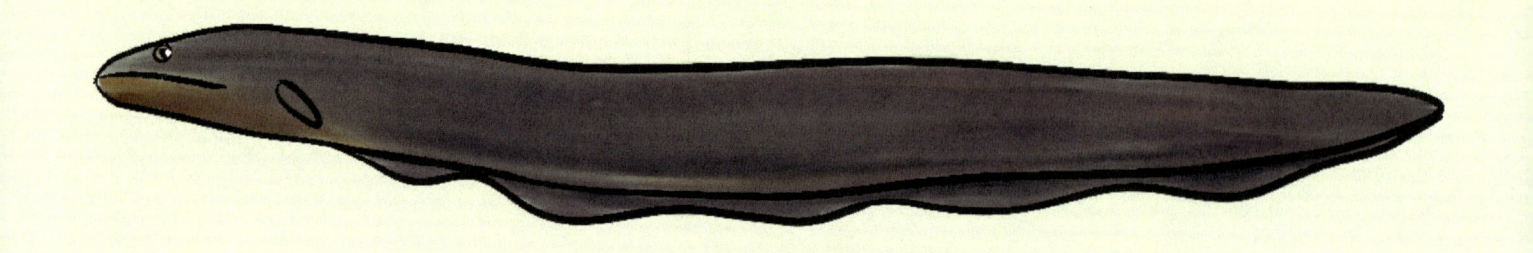

E IS FOR EEL,
THIS ONE IS
ELECTRIC!

F

F is for flying fish, they can be very hectic.

G

G IS FOR GAR,
THEY HAVE A VERY
LONG SNOUT.

H

H IS FOR HOOK.
IT'S SHARP –
WATCH OUT!

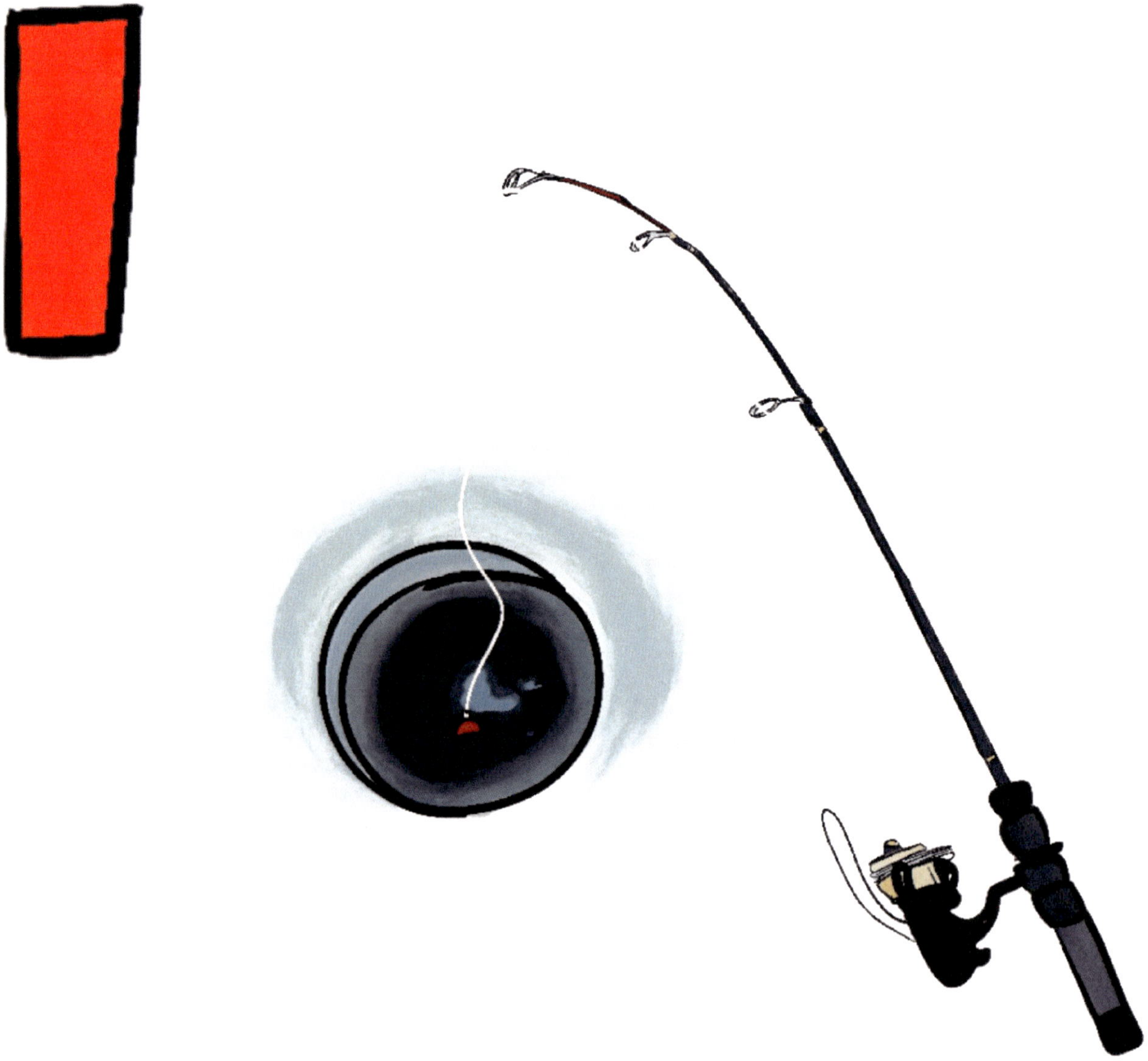

I IS FOR
ICE FISHING,
IN THE FREEZING
COLD.

J

J IS FOR JIG,
KNOWN AS A
"MONEY BAIT"
AROUND THE GLOBE.

K

K IS FOR
KAYAK FISHING,
MY DAD'S FAVORITE
WAY TO FISH.

L

L IS FOR LURE, INVENTED BY JAMES HEDDON.

M

M IS FOR MARLIN,
MORE POWERFUL
THAN ANY OTHER
FISH IN THE SEA!

N

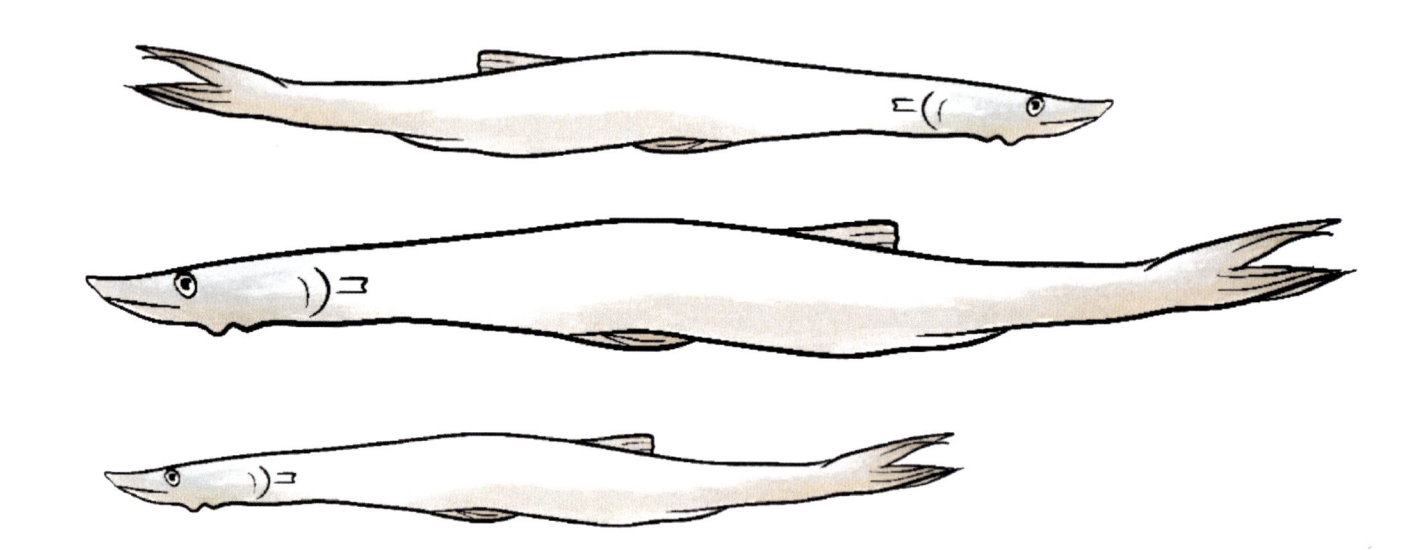

N IS FOR NOODLEFISH, LIKE THE PASTA I LIKE TO EAT.

O

O IS FOR OYSTER,
THEY GROW
PEARLS INSIDE.

P

P IS FOR PERCH,
THEY TRAVEL IN
SCHOOLS BUT
AREN'T BIG IN SIZE.

Q

Q IS FOR
QUEEN TRIGGERFISH,
IT IS TRUE ROYALTY.

R

R IS FOR
ROD AND REEL,
IF YOU'RE FISHING
THOSE ARE TOOLS
YOU'LL NEED.

S

S is for stingray, sunfish, and shrimp.

T

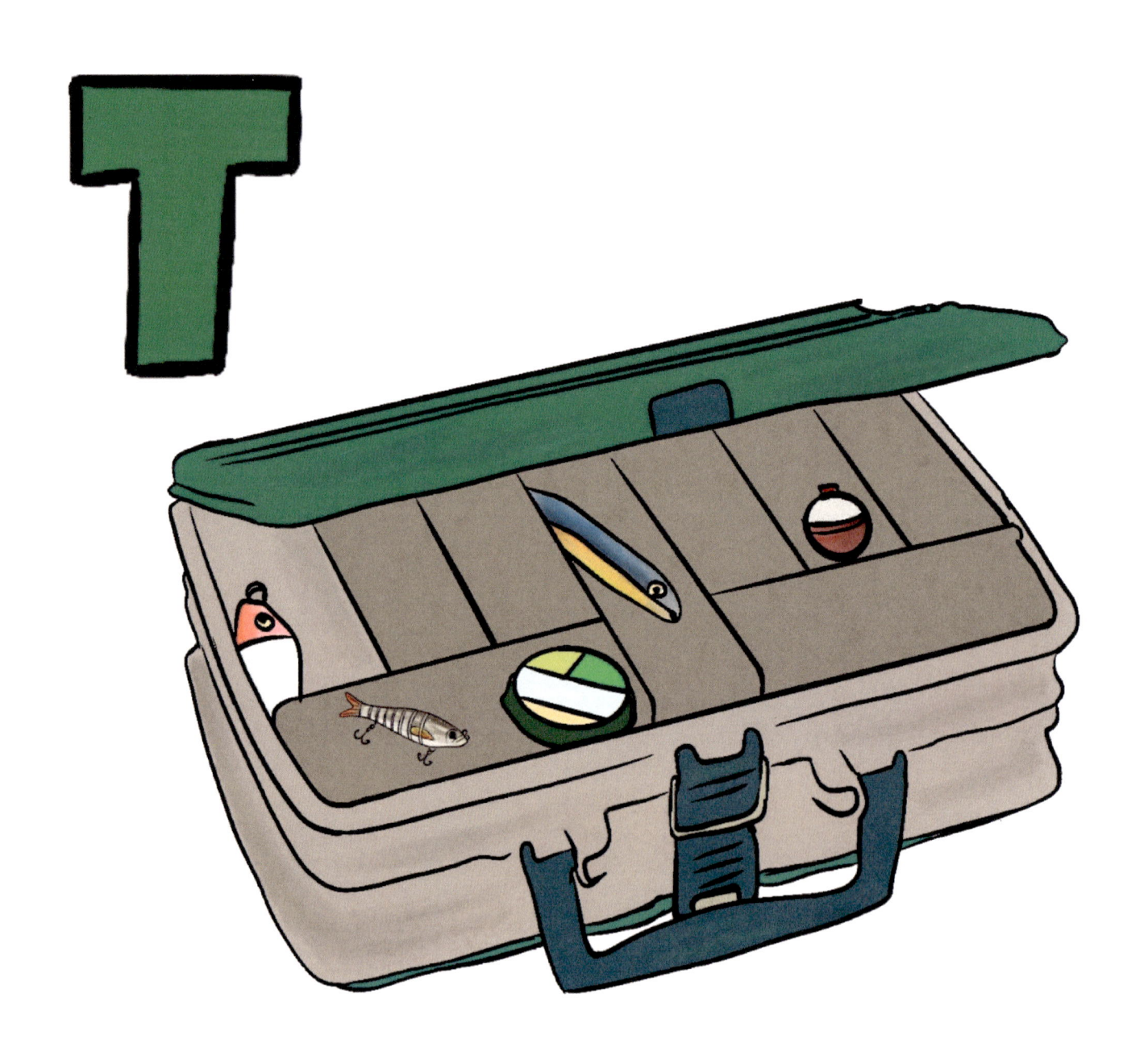

T IS FOR TACKLE BOX, MY MOST TREASURED TOOL KIT.

U

U IS FOR UNICORN FISH,
I BET THAT CAUGHT
YOU BY SURPRISE!

V

V IS FOR VEST,
FOR SAFETY AND
TO ORGANIZE.

W

W IS FOR WADERS, THAT KEEP ME WARM AND DRY.

X

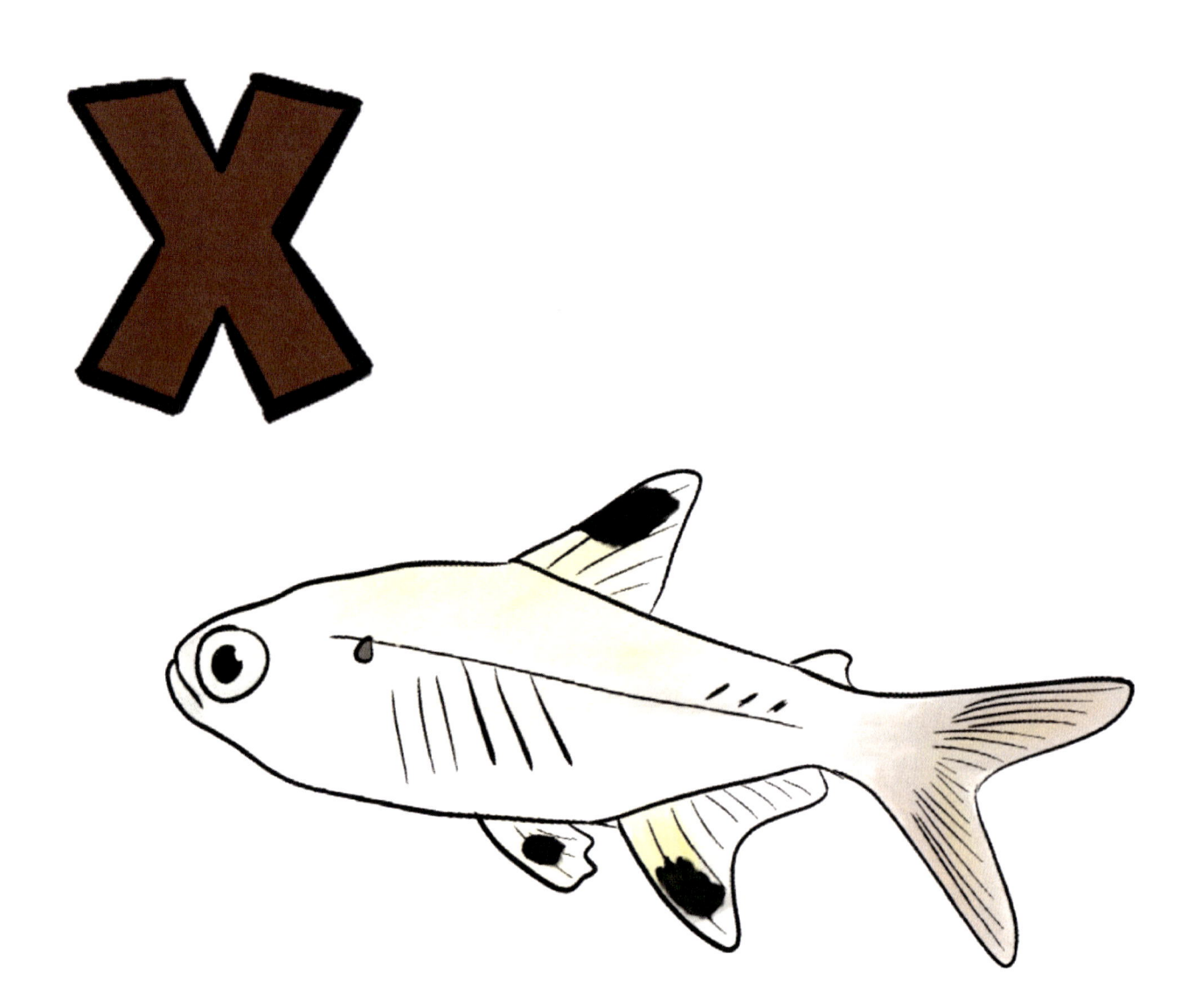

X IS FOR X-RAY FISH, THAT I HAVEN'T SEEN WITH MY OWN TWO EYES.

Y

Y IS FOR YELLOWFIN TUNA, BUT TUNA COMES IN OTHER SHAPES AND SIZES.

z

Z IS FOR ZEBRA FISH,
I REALLY LIKE THE
STRIPES!

THE END.

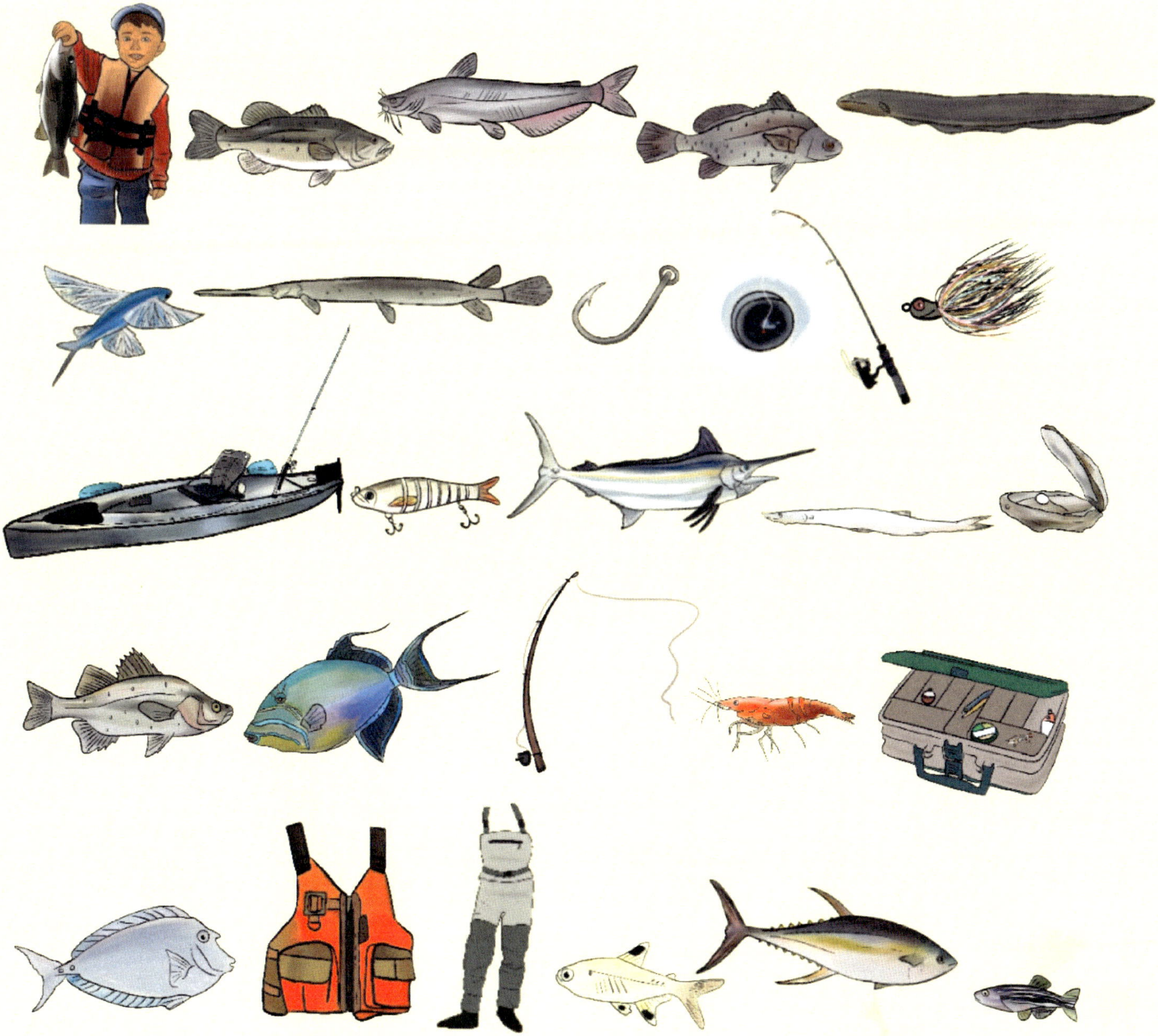

THE FISHING SONG

GOING FISHING, TO CATCH A FISH
CATCHING IS A FISH IS ON MY LIST
F-I-S-H-I-N-G
BOY DO I LOVE FI-I-SHING!

GOTTA BE QUIET, SET THE HOOK!
REEL HIM IN AND TAKE A GOOD LOOK!
F-I-S-H-I-N-G
BOY DO I LOVE FI-I-SHING!